The Berenstain Bears'
MAD, MAD, MAD
TOY CRAZE

When little bears want
the same toys as their friends,
they may hook into a craze
that just never ends.

A First Time Book®

BROWN BEAR

MOUSTACHE C...

BOW BEAR

HAT CAT

WIG PIG

FUNNY BUNNY

HAIRY HARRY

PURPLE COW

PUNK SKUNK

FURR...

...ERRY

SQUIRM WORM

SNAKE EYES

LUCKY BEAR

DINO RHINO

PACHY DERM

FOGGY FROGGY

DROOP SNOOT

HORN BILL

STARE BEAR

ROAD TOAD

CLOCK BEAR

FAT CAT

BROWN COW

QUEEN BEAR

KING BEAR

HONEY BUNNY

BOG FROG

SCARE BEAR

LUCY GOOSIE

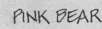

PINK BEAR

DORK STORK

The Berenstain Bears'

MAD, MAD, MAD TOY CRAZE

Stan & Jan Berenstain

Random House 🏠 New York

Copyright © 1999 by Berenstain Enterprises, Inc. All rights reserved under
International and Pan-American Copyright Conventions. Published in the United
States by Random House, Inc., New York, and simultaneously in Canada by
Random House of Canada Limited, Toronto.
www.randomhouse.com/kids www.berenstainbears.com
Library of Congress Cataloging-in-Publication Data: Berenstain, Stan, 1923-
The Berenstain Bears' mad, mad, mad toy craze / Stan & Jan Berenstain.   p. cm. —
(First time books) SUMMARY: Brother and Sister Bear get caught up buying as many
of the popular new Beary Bubbies as they can.   ISBN 0-679-88958-2 (trade). —
ISBN 0-679-98958-7 (lib. bdg.) 1. Bears—Fiction.   2. Toys—Fiction.
3. Fads—Fiction.] I. Berenstain, Jan, 1923-   . II. Title.   III. Series: Berenstain,
Stan, 1923- . First time books.   PZ7.B4483Beml 1999   [E]—dc21 98-36353
Printed in the United States of America 10 9 8 7 6 5 4 3 2 1

It was a calm and peaceful afternoon in Bear Country. It was calm and peaceful outside the Bear family's tree house, where the tulips were blooming and the grass was growing.

It was calm and peaceful inside the tree house, where Papa Bear was reading the afternoon paper and Mama Bear was checking out the TV schedule.

But it was all over for peace and calm when
Brother and Sister came tearing home. They rushed
up the front steps and burst into the living room all
excited and so out of breath they could hardly talk.

"Papa...Mama," they gasped. "We need it...we gotta have it...we absolutely gotta—"
"Now, hold everything," said Papa. "Just calm down and tell me just what it is that you need and absolutely gotta have."

"An advance!" sputtered Brother.

"That's right," gasped Sister. "An advance on our allowance. And if we don't get it, Herb's Hobby Shop is gonna run out!"

"Going to run out of what?" asked Papa.

"Why, Beary Bubbies, of course!" said Sister.

"And what, may I ask, are Boony Bearies, Booby Bubbies—whatever that was you said?" asked Papa.

"Beary Bubbies, Papa," said Brother. "They're terrific! They're great! They're fabulous!"

"And they're cute and adorable!" said Sister. "And each one is different and each one has its own name."

"Cousin Fred already has six of 'em!" said Brother.

"Lizzy has eight and Queenie has ten!" said Sister.

"Well," said Papa, reaching for his wallet and taking out some money, "far be it from me to deprive my cubs of Booby Bearies."

The money and the cubs disappeared so fast you'd have thought it was a magic act. "Well," said a bewildered Papa, "what do you suppose *that* was about?"

"Come to think of it," said Mama, "I did see a sign on Herb's Hobby Shop's window. It said 'We have Beary Bubbies—$2.95!' I didn't think much about it. But I suppose that's what the cubs are talking about."

"*Talking about* is putting it mildly," said Papa. "They were flipping out about it. They were through the roof about it." He sighed. "It's just amazing to me," he said as he went back to his paper, "how otherwise sensible cubs can get pulled into any silly thing that comes along."

"I suppose," said Mama as she went back to the TV schedule.

The cubs ran all the way to Herb's Hobby Shop

holding their precious Beary Bubby money

in their hot little hands.

HERB'S HOBBY SHOP

WE HAVE
BEARY
BUBBIES!
$2.95

And lucky cubs that they were, they got there in time to buy the last three Beary Bubbies in the store. "When do you expect more?" asked Brother.

"I can't say," said Herb. "I can't even get them on the phone. It's busy 24 hours a day."

Though it was true that Cousin Fred had six, Lizzy had eight, and Queenie had ten Beary Bubbies, while Brother and Sister had only three, the ones they had were really cute. Each one was different from the other and each one had its very own name.

HAIRY HARRY

ZIGGY ZIPPO

DIMPLE DARLING

Back home, Sister said, "We'd like to introduce our Beary Bubbies. This one is named Ziggy Zippo, this one is named Dimple Darling—"

"And this one is named Hairy Harry," said Brother.

"Hmm," said Papa as they all sat down to dinner.

"They *are* kind of cute," said Mama.

The next day, the cubs came to Papa with a proposition. "We won't ask for any more advances on our allowance if you'll hire us to do chores," said Brother.

"What are you going to do with the money you earn?" asked Papa.

"Buy more Beary Bubbies, of course," said Sister.

"But you said Herb's Hobby Shop is out of them and can't get more," said Papa.

"That's right," said Brother. "But Lizzy has two of a kind and she's willing to sell one for $5.00."

"So does Queenie," said Sister. "Only she wants $7.00."

"Hey," said Papa. "I thought they were just $2.95 at Herb's Hobby Shop."

"That's right," said Sister. "Only Herb's all out."

"Hmm," said Papa. "Buying and selling Beary Bubbies is beginning to sound like a pretty good business."

"Speaking of business," said Mama, "here's a piece in the paper about a fellow who bought a whole bunch of Beary Bubbies before they became popular. It says here that he just sold his entire collection for a fortune."

"Lemme see that!" said Papa, snatching the paper.
"Papa," said Brother. "About those chores?"

For the next couple of days,
Brother and Sister pulled weeds,

sorted trash,

and cleaned out cobwebs like there was no tomorrow.

Of course, there *were* more tomorrows— lots of them. And Brother and Sister were determined to spend them figuring out ways to get more Beary Bubbies.

"Just listen to this," said Papa, reading from a *Beary Bubbies* magazine he had found at the supermarket. "A rare Beary Bubby was sold in Bearville for hundreds of dollars! Did you hear that? Hundreds of dollars!"

That's when Brother and Sister burst in with the Beary Bubbies they had bought with their chore money. "Papa!" cried Brother. "We heard a rumor that the TOYS IZ US store in Big Bear City just got a shipment of Beary Bubbies!"

"A *huge* shipment!" cried Sister.

"Jump in the car!" cried Papa.
"But Big Bear City is twenty miles away," said Mama, following them out the door.

By the time Mama finished her sentence, Papa and the cubs were off in a cloud of dust.

"Look! A skywriter!" cried Sister as they roared along the road to Big Bear City.

"What does it say?" asked Papa.

"It says BEARY BUBBIES FOREVER!" said Brother.

"We'd better hurry," cried Papa, flooring the gas pedal, "or TOYS IZ US might run out!"

The rumor about TOY IZ US turned out to be true. A huge banner said WE HAVE BEARY BUBBIES—$5! It looked like a big Beary Bubby party.

Only it was more like a big aggravation. The lines wound around the store, babies were crying, and two daddies got into a shoving match about a place in line and had to be taken away by the police.

But the cubs got their Beary Bubbies. In fact, they headed home up to their necks in them.

Of course, not many things are forever—
and Beary Bubbies certainly weren't. Pretty
soon, Beary Bubbies were everywhere. They
came in Krinkly Krumbles cereal boxes.

You could get them at the
gas station with a fill-up.

You could get them with a
Krazy Meal at the Burger Bear. After
a while, just about everybody in Bear Country
had so many Beary Bubbies that they didn't
know what to do with them.

There wasn't much you *could* do with them in the first place. You couldn't play dolly with them the way you could with a good doll.

You couldn't play choo-choo with them the way you could with a toy train.

You couldn't play baseball with them the way you could with a bat and ball.

All you could do was look at them—except they had a way of looking back at you and making you think about all the money you had spent on them.

The only thing you could really do with them
is brag about how many you had.

And no matter how many you had,
there was always somebody who had more.